Love
and
Kisses

To my editor, Mary Lee Donovan, with valentines!
— S. W.

To Mary Lee Donovan and Anne Moore with thanks
— M. S.

ISBN 0-439-18783-4

Text copyright © 1999 by Sarah Wilson.
Illustrations copyright © 1999 by Melissa Sweet.
All rights reserved.
Published by Scholastic Inc.,
555 Broadway, New York, NY 10012,
by arrangement with Candlewick Press.
SCHOLASTIC and associated logos are trademarks
and/or registered trademarks of Scholastic Inc.

12 11 10 9 8 7 6 5 4 3 2   1 2 3 4 5 6/0

Printed in the U.S.A.   23

First Scholastic printing, January 2001

This book was typeset in Lemonade.
The pictures were done in watercolor,
gouache, and collage.

Love and Kisses

Sarah Wilson

illustrated by
Melissa Sweet

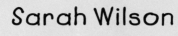

SCHOLASTIC INC.

New York Toronto London Auckland Sydney
Mexico City New Delhi Hong Kong

Blow a kiss and let it go,

You never know how love will grow—

Smooch
and smack!
You kiss your cat.

Your cat may kiss a cow.

The cow may kiss a giggling goose,

the goose, a fish—somehow!

The fish **splish!** **splash!** may kiss a fox.

The fox may kiss a frog.

The frog may jump to plant a kiss

upon a friendly dog.

The dog may kiss a frisky horse

and catch him by surprise!

The horse may kiss a red-winged bird

with twinkles in her eyes.

The bird may fly to kiss a cow,
who'll laugh a great big

The cow may run to kiss a cat,

who'll then kiss . . .

you-know-who!

Kisses! Kisses!

Smooch and SMACK!

You'll have your love
    and kisses back!